Flying Kites

Gautam N Ramachandran

Ukiyoto Publishing

All global publishing rights are held by

Ukiyoto Publishing

Published in 2022

Content Copyright © **Gautam N Ramachandran**

ISBN 9789364946995

All rights reserved.
No part of this publication may be reproduced, transmitted, or stored in a retrieval system, in any form by any means, electronic, mechanical, photocopying, recording or otherwise, without the prior permission of the publisher.

The moral rights of the author have been asserted.

This book is sold subject to the condition that it shall not by way of trade or otherwise, be lent, resold, hired out or otherwise circulated, without the publisher's prior consent, in any form of binding or cover other than that in which it is published.

www.ukiyoto.com

To my mother

Acknowledgement

I thank God for watching over me all the while. Writing a book is a sustained process and more rewarding than I could have ever imagined. None of this would have been possible without my wife, Ciny. My creativity could come to fruition only because of the comfortable space she created for me. My mother-in-law Prasanna S Pillai, who herself is a writer, is the inspiration for me to translate my thoughts into words. I am forever thankful to them for letting me loose on this literary trail.

I want to thank my brothers, Rahul and Nikhil, for their constant support and encouragement. Being avid and voracious readers themselves, they are probably the best critics I could have ever asked for.

I am eternally grateful to two of my Dad's distinguished colleagues Dr William Selvamurthy and Dr Jaganmohan Wadhawan, who provided me with valuable inputs regarding his role as a Scientist.

If there was somebody who influenced my writings, it is my teacher and guru, Professor Dr. C S Jayaram. I am indebted to him for all those beautiful lectures – a springboard to my creativity..

I would like to pay my special regards to everyone at Ukiyoto Publishing and I am honored to be a part of your team which has helped me bring this memoir to life.

Finally, my deepest gratitude to all those who believed in me when I decided to tread the path of the many wonderful writers out there.

Contents

-Chapter 1-	1
-Chapter 2-	2
-Chapter 3-	3
-Chapter 4-	4
-Chapter 5-	5
-Chapter 6-	6
-Chapter 7-	8
-Chapter 8-	9
-Chapter 9-	10
-Chapter 10-	12
-Chapter 11-	14
-Chapter 12-	15
-Chapter 13-	16
-Chapter 14-	17
-Chapter 15-	18
-Chapter 16-	19
-Chapter 17-	20
-Chapter 18-	21
-Chapter 19-	22
-Chapter 20-	24
About the Author	25

-Chapter 1-

Dad was not a workaholic but he was passionate about his job. I remember him quite often proudly remarking that he was a Central Government servant. There was a certain amount of joy or pride when he said that. I remember him coming back from the office in the evenings after work but never saw him go to the office in the mornings as he would have left long before we woke up. The formative years of my life, the early 1980s were the best days of my life. As is with everyone that is one stage where one experiences moments that remain etched forever in one's memory. We were Bangaloreans then. I was born in Allahabad and brought up in Bangalore and so though a native of Kerala I could identify myself with the culture of Karnataka, the place I grew up in. In fact, that affinity is still within me as I am haunted by all those wonderful memories of my early childhood.

Dad was a Scientist at I.A.M (Institute of Aerospace Medicine), Bangalore. That's the only thing I knew about his profession then. I and my brothers were busy growing up in Kendriya Vidyalaya Hebbal. Life was beautiful and all our needs as children were taken care of. There was one particular incident that I still remember. We had friends of our age in the neighbourhood and I particularly remember this boy Ashwin, and we did everything together those days. We used to play a lot of indoor board games and 'Scrabble' was one such interesting game that we spent a lot of time on. The board games belonged to Ashwin so after every game he used to take it back home. I and my brothers asked Dad to buy us this game. For some reason he refused. We were so upset with this denial that we made this board with available materials at home. A complete DIY. Maybe this act moved Dad and Mom so much that without wasting any time he bought us this game. As wonderful parents, they very much understood our needs. This might have been a very trivial incident in my life but for some reason, it remains within me as fresh as it was - a stark example of good parenting.

-Chapter 2-

Dad was a voracious reader and there were about thousands of books he brought from his office library. They were stacked in cardboard cartons. The majority of those books were fiction in almost every kind of genre. It was only post his retirement in the late 1990s that he had switched to non-fiction. I was never attracted to Dad's collection of books. My older brother like my Dad was engrossed in those books and was so addicted to them that he carried with him everywhere the novels he had been reading.

It was during those days that something interested me very much – kite flying. We used to get kites from the nearby shop and when they were unavailable, we designed our own types. On the terrace, we waited for the right thrust of the wind to launch our kite and when we did, it was such an out of the world experience. It all seemed that you had established a connection with the sky and the interest was such that I never wanted to let go of the flying kite because I was being led into an entirely unknown realm of the blue sky. A particular thought process initiated within me that seemed to take me away from this real-world to another imaginary space which kept my thoughts reeling in introspection. Maybe it was at this point in time I could come to terms and reason with the realities of life. While I steered clear of invading kites my thoughts exuberantly worked on. A lot of images of my Dad passed through me. Perhaps I could understand why he was busy and I assumed, professionally he did carry a lot on his shoulders. I understood why he did not take us to the movie 'First Blood'. The day he said we would take us for this film he suffered a heart attack and was admitted to the hospital. I was shattered then as I missed the movie but later on in life, once as I was guiding my kite higher I could feel the human emotions that I may have lacked then.

-Chapter 3-

Dad used to make it a point that all of us got an opportunity to spend time outdoors. As is with any middle-class family of any day, going to the cinemas, shopping, dining out etc. were routines in our life. During one of my thoughtful odysseys with my kite sky high, I realized that Dad was indeed making up for the professional time and space by giving us quality time at home. He probably wanted to make sure we were not left behind as he soared in his official duties.

I got this opportunity once during my 4th standard when we had a holiday for school. Dad asked me to go along with him to his office. It was an unforgettable experience as I got to know something about the place to which my Dad had been so attached. Not all people love the profession they are into. For Dad, being an employee of the government was sacrosanct. When I was there at his workplace, a particular condemned fighter aircraft caught my attention. Since the place he worked was closely associated with the Indian Air Force there were many such aircraft on display at various places. This plane was close to my Dad's desk. He gave me the go-ahead to climb up the stairs to the cockpit of the plane. I noticed the aircraft all roughed up as I took the pilot seat. I don't recollect how long I remained seated there but the thrill of the moment is still fresh in me. I envied all those pilots who could guide such machines like kites into space. It gave me that push to transcend from everything that is worldly to a more sublime and peaceful disposition. Basically, it was a transformation of sorts and immediately I was in all awe of my Dad for that experience.

-Chapter 4-

I never got another chance to visit Dad's workplace after that, but that one moment of joy I experienced, matured my mind to a great extent. Though he was a civilian, what gave him the ultimate satisfaction was that he was working towards the Defence-related needs of the nation. This I realized, though in a small way after being at his workplace.

School vacations were big breaks. This was a time when we got to see our own people who till then were connected to us through the postal department, way back in the 1980s – a time when relationships had a different meaning. I remember one such summer vacation when all of us visited my mother's native home in Kottayam, Kerala. Those journeys back to our roots are still fresh in my mind for strange reasons. On one such memorable trip, we took the Bangalore express to Kerala and Dad had booked a First Class compartment for just the 5 of us. Dad and mom kept talking of different matters, my older brother was busy reading novels as usual and my younger brother was cuddled in Mom's lap. He is always a mummy's boy. I enjoyed being at the window side of the coupe. As the train tore through the night, I followed the moon in the sky and as usual, my mind wandered into thoughts. Though all the others had sound sleep I just enjoyed moving along with the sights in the night sky. I did not want to miss that wonderful experience of the starry night and almost unending borders of the Western Ghats.

-Chapter 5-

We reached my mother's village in Kottayam, Kerala the next day. It was only then I realized that there were so many people within our family circle. The loving grandparents, aunts, uncles, cousins, a three legged dog named 'Shankar', a few kittens, a cow and its little one, hens and all these surrounded by lush green vegetation – and there was harmony. The two months we spent there were days of utmost joy. Being city bred, the sights and sound of the village was soothing to the senses. I can never recollect anything about Dad and never missed him during those days because there were so many people to look after us. He had gone back to Bangalore.

After two months of absolute tranquility the vacation had come to an end. It was heart-breaking to leave. That peaceful coexistence with nature, the beautiful sights and sound, the love of our grandparents, it all seemed that you were transposed from the hustle and bustle of Bangalore days to a soul enriching experience. As we were on our journey back to Bangalore, just one thing occupied my mind. Almost all the relatives we spent our time with were from my mother's side. We just met a few people from my Dad's side. This puzzled me but I did not let it bother me too much as I was relishing the memories of the vacation that went by. Unlike before my mind was filled with unbounded joy. My brothers too felt rejuvenated. This seemed to be another very important lesson in good parenting – going back to our roots. Gazing at the night sky I felt my thoughts were richer than before but I missed all my new found relatives. I had a sea change in my thoughts as the Island Express took us back to the Kannada land.

-Chapter 6-

Dad was always particular that his busy schedule did not affect other members of his family. He made it a point that we got adequate family time and so going out to the movies or shopping happened quite often. Lal Bagh, Commercial Street, Majestic, Kamath Hotel were some of our weekly haunts. One incident which was a big emotional let-down for me was when we were at a Cinema hall watching the super hit movie, "Ek Duje Ke Liye". Towards interval, Dad complained of breathlessness and we discontinued the show and went home and of course, we were disappointed perhaps not because of Dad's health but because we could not complete the movie. I have always been fond of the Silver screen. There were rich moments too in our movie-going experience. We watched the country's first 3D film, "My Dear Kuttichaathan" (Tamil version). "Gandhi" was another gem of a movie that we watched together. While all this kept happening Dad was also very sincere in his profession.

Until very late in life, little did I know that he was an accomplished Scientist. The only moment I thought about Dad's work-life balance was when I had been alone intently looking at the emptiness of the sky from our house in Yeshwanthpur. This seemingly unending mysterious space of our universe gets intriguing the longer you work your thoughts around it. My soliloquies were more profound and rightly understood when I let lose my vision into this emptiness.

Dad did not enforce strict rules for studies at home like many parents. Instead, he would occasionally check on our academic progress. It was during the VI standard; I was given my progress report from the school and which had to be signed by Dad or Mom. I did not want to show it immediately at home so hid it under the bookshelf. After a few days, this was found and Dad was furious. He called me to his room and unleashed his anger with his belt. One of those lashes missed its mark and the metal buckle piece of that belt hit the bridge of my nose and I started bleeding. Dad immediately threw the belt aside and took me to the local medical clinic. I was administered first aid and both of us returned home in complete peace. Dad has never physically hurt any of us since then. As far as the wound on the bridge of my nose is concerned, it is my identification mark on my face in all official documents.

-Chapter 7-

Playing cricket, board games, reading comic books were some of the pastimes we indulged in during the holidays. One thing that I especially enjoyed doing was making kites and flying them or rather trying to fly them. There was a shop nearby that sold such essential kids' items and we would get the kites from there. If we didn't get it there we would just make it on our own.

Those days on any day in our locality if we looked up the sky during the daytime we could see many kites trying to make their mark up there. I enjoyed being in control of a kite that was sky high and unlike many others, I would have held it swinging for an entire day. I was unaware or never really thought as to why this fascinated me so much. My friends would either try to snap someone else's kite or let their own loose after some time. The sight of these kites in flight set my mind in motion and it seemed that all things past and present reverberated within me. I was lost in conversation with the unknown.

There were moments when I felt annoyed with Dad and sometimes love and respect knew no bounds. Television has always been an integral part of our household and no matter what the program was, it was always kept switched on. Doordarshan was to telecast a late-night popular English movie titled "Escape to Victory" and all of us waited eagerly for it. Just a few hours before the movie was supposed to start, our Nelco television stopped functioning. The local technician was called who declared the TV unfit. So the feeling that Dad could not do anything to get another TV unsettled my highly immature mind. Not long after that in the early months of 1986 Dad brought home a Solidaire colour TV just before the World Cup Football. When Dad kept fulfilling our wishes, I looked up at him as someone who would never falter and when I look back in time today I must say, he never did.

-Chapter 8-

Dad was already a CVD patient and he used inhalers when he had breathing issues. The Bangalore climate was not at all congenial for his health. In the year 1987, we broke all ties with Bangalore as he got transferred to Kochi. It was heart-breaking to leave the school and friends and again my inner voice seemed to say that Dad should not have done this. We finally moved to Kerala, a place that would literally transform my thoughts and my life.

We got admission to KendriyaVidyalayaErnakulam. Initial days were tough as it was a new place - friends, teachers and also the communication part, viz. Malayalam. As we were brought up in Bangalore, it was difficult to cope up with the language initially. Dad was at Naval Base and heading Naval Psychological Research Unit there. In no time we were able to cope up with the new environment and we enjoyed it. Though Dad had moved to Kochi to improve his health conditions, all was not that good. Very soon he was in consultations with top cardiologists for his ill health.

In spite of all this, I could see Dad's zeal in official duties. He used to travel to DRDO Delhi for important meetings. I became more observant and slowly began to realize that he was a very important person in a top-notch Central Government job. Though Kochi was not a metro like Bangalore, it had a cosmopolitan outlook and we could quickly adapt to the change. My outlook on my Dad gradually took shape in my mature mind. Though I never got a chance to fly kites in the changing times my thoughts always took flight and I enjoyed it. Perhaps in my deepest thoughts, my Dad occupied my mind foremost.

-Chapter 9-

Dad always moved with the times and kept himself updated on all events across the world. There was not one topic that he could not talk or debate about. He was an encyclopaedia who could expound at any length about any topic under the sun. He never forced us, brothers, into any particular career but he was there to guide us in our strides where ever it led to.

He always spoke highly of the life and discipline in the nation's Defence forces and basically, he would have liked one of us to pursue that career but he never said so. I remember one instance before I passed out of 12th standard that a career in the National Defence Academy is one of the best options right upfront after my school education. At that moment I felt it was just a passing remark or suggestion and as ignorant as I could be, I just brushed aside such thoughts. Even if I had wished for a career in NDA it was not easy at all as the entrance tests and interviews make it a hard nut to crack even today.

Dad would read the newspapers thoroughly and cut out articles or editorials from it which might be of future referential use for all of us. He also made notes on various aspects of the country's progress like the GDP, Science and Technology, Medicine, the backwardness of the downtrodden in our society and other distinctive topics which mattered to the nation as a whole. He was a storehouse of knowledge, waiting to be tapped.

The only common factor thought wise between me and my Dad was our love for the sky, planets, stars and deep space. My interest was purely instinctive but he had a thorough subject knowledge and moreover, those came under his realm of study professionally. I later came to know that he was a Scientist in Space Psychology and had a role to play in the selection of Indian Cosmonauts for space research in the early 1980s during his stint at the Institute of Aerospace Medicine, Bangalore.

There was one thing about him that I was sure of, that he loved his profession much more than anything else. Of course, he was there for all of us. To every enquiry regarding my Dad's profession, I would just say, "Scientist." I never took any interest to know more about what he really did. I always had a feeling that he was unable to strike a balance between official and family life. I felt there was an absence of emotional connectedness.

-Chapter 10-

As we moved into our college-going days that kind of a feeling grew within me until one day we came to understand that Mom was diagnosed with a Giant Cell Tumour on her right shoulder. That was a turning point in all our lives. One of those days as I was travelling to Chennai from Kochi by train, looking at the night sky and pondering over the turn of events, I realised the personal side of Dad. From the moment we came to know that my mom was a cancer patient, he dedicated his whole self to looking after her medical needs.

My mother had to undergo various surgeries at different hospitals in Kochi, Thiruvananthapuram and Chennai and all the while this person, my Dad stood strong and stood along. None of us brothers realised the intensity of the medical procedures that were being followed. Since we were in our college days, Dad didn't reveal much of how the treatment had been going.

That night when I was travelling by train to Chennai in a second class compartment and seated by the window side my mind wandered into the night sky and I felt myself just floating up there like a kite. I began to realise this part of my Dad I never knew. It was intense and a revelation.

After years of medical worries, mom was stable. Surgeries, transplantation, radiation, chemotherapy and the pain, everything had come to an end. My mom was able to get back to normal life but with very limited movements of her affected right hand. For Dad it was just a minor medical need taken care of and that there was nothing to worry about henceforth. I could not fathom what my parents actually went through.

Very soon my Dad retired from service. None of us anticipated this as he never told us. Maybe only mom knew it. One fine evening as I came back from college, I saw him happy with some flower bouquets. He told that he had retired but for me, I could not digest what it really meant. I perceived retirement as an inevitable stage that one needs to go through as age catches up and so this was just normal.

It was years later that I realised what it really meant to retire from service, especially if one had really loved what one was doing professionally all the while. Dad was considered for a two year period extension initially but due to some political events in the country during that time it did not happen. Instead, he was given a private project at Mumbai which he did not continue for long. Probably nothing else, however lucrative it may be could have satisfied him more than what he was doing as a Scientist.

-Chapter 11-

It was only later in life in my silent thoughts that I really came to terms with reality. Maybe it's the same with everyone. With maturity, your thought process changes and thereby your interpretation about the whole life itself. After retirement, Dad was completely engaged in reading. Unlike earlier days the kind of books he read also changed. Fiction no more interested him. He was keener on genres like psychology, human physiology, space, medicine and sociology among the many.

In fact, every moment of one's interaction with him was a learning process. I regret having not done that. He never asserted his interests upon us and unfortunately, the youth in me was never inspired by his high erudition which is definitely a big miss for me.

Years later at Panambur beach in Mangalore, my thoughts were taking me back in time. The annual international kite festival was on. Kites of different shapes and sizes were all set to conquer the sky. Like always that was one extravaganza that I could not afford to miss. The higher each kite soared the deeper I moved in my thoughts.

After marriage and moving to Mangalore I was away from home for quite some time. Through the emails from my Dad, I could sense his failing health. I could make out that he had totally distanced himself from what he loved the most, the scientific temper. He seemed to enjoy the quiet times with mom, though health was an issue for both. My brothers and their families also moved out on job demands and our parents were to themselves for some time. This had always been a concern for all of us then and wished to get back home as early as possible.

-Chapter 12-

When I was in Mangalore, I was more mature and so could clearly see through things while I reflected on past events. It was such a shame that I was unable to draw on the resources of my Dad when there was an opportunity.

Dad never craved power or recognition as he was a very humble person. His life and career were knowledge-driven. He never claimed any rights of his ancestral place while he was pursuing higher studies. He was willing to forsake it for his siblings and this was done with utmost humility. It was through sheer merit that he went places and could have a remarkable career. There were murmurs in his native home that he never looked back or came after he left for higher studies. Well, it was his passion to acquire more knowledge and to excel in his profession that he had to forsake those formalities. As they say, knowledge knows no boundaries.

Getting back home whenever we could be one of the priciest moments in life. After many years of Mangalore life, we returned to Kochi. Dad and mom had become one as is with all elderly couples in the later phase of their lives. Unlike before there was a change in my interaction with Dad. I was overjoyed in returning to my parents' side. Unlike before I wanted to establish a good connection with my Dad. We discussed in detail the official and personal happenings till that date. It was relieving. For the first time, I was all ears to Dad's perspective on the things that happened around during our absence. It was not that I never listened to him earlier. This time around I was keen on getting more information about Dad's colleagues and about how he was spending his retired life. Probably my curiosity was not just objective but rather it was an emotional utterance. I understood how much I really missed them over the years. I understood one thing about Dad that day, that he was not only a great person in all aspects, but he was also a bundle of nobilities. From then on I had a sort of mature relationship with Dad. It was overwhelming and long due.

-Chapter 13-

My mom and dad shared a very unique bond and that was a beautiful sight to see. They were quite healthy to work around with their daily needs. From then on all of us made it a point that we got together frequently and secured an unmissable bond.

Very soon Dad's health started declining. Our visits to the hospital became more frequent. It was not that serious initially and no in-depth evaluation was done as the Doctors were of the opinion that it was just the age factor and also because he was already on various medicines for heart disease, blood pressure and diabetes for several years. Basically, he led a sedentary life and probably that twisted the scale against us. What kept him going was his strong will and positivity. He was not willing to get cowed down by illnesses of any kind. He was an atheist but an optimist. Even today, as I recollect the early days, I feel the vacuum in our lives left by Dad.

In Kerala, Onam and Vishu are two days of festivities Malayalees celebrate. The celebrations are so rich that they instill in us the spirit of oneness. Dad never compromised on the happiness shrouding these festivities. Normally a week before the festival he would plan all the required shopping and set the tone for the celebrations. 'Sadya' being the main attraction on these days, he would insist on preparing as many dishes as possible and would lead the show from the front. Those times we never understood the reason for the frenzy but today I miss all that. Probably then we did not understand the essence of why Dad wanted to celebrate these festivals in absolute mirth. As I look back, I realise that it was a lesson for all of us - enshrining the true spirit of the family.

-Chapter 14-

Dads health worsened all of a sudden and he was diagnosed with a non-alcoholic liver haemorrhage. We admitted him to Amrita Institute of Medical Sciences (AIMS), Kochi. His creatinine was on the higher side and after weeks of medical care, he could come back home. Not long after this, one fine morning he suddenly showed signs of unrest and became difficult to manage. We took him to AIMS again and this time he required longer hospitalisation.

The danger that was there to his life was explained to us by the Head of the Department and his team of Gastroenterologists at the hospital. Those days we were basically shuttling to and fro between home and hospital. Another thing I noticed was my mom's care and concern for my ailing Dad. When I looked at this from a different perspective, it was mom's chance in life to repay in kindness he never-say-die attitude and grit of Dad when he dedicated his time and space to provide her with the best medical care when she was badly hit by the tumour on her shoulder. As I pondered over these in my sweet silent thoughts, I could only thank God for the beautiful relationship that existed between Dad and Mom – it was remarkable.

-Chapter 15-

In spite of failing health Dad never compromised on keeping himself updated on other happenings around the world. He continued being that voracious reader of those days on varied subjects. In fact there was a sea change in his choice of books that he read. During his early days, Dad's favourite writers were Alistair MacLean, Irving Wallace, Robert Ludlum and many more in the thriller and adventure genre. Towards the end of his life, he was keener on books on the philosophy of life, science and technology, space research, medicine, Buddhism and many more of such writings that reflected on man's position on planet earth – his quintessential subject matter. Basically, he was more inclined to the theories on space psychology. He would talk endlessly on this and that cheered him up even when he was struggling in the hospital.

I got to understand his likes and dislikes more profoundly during those days. He would tirelessly talk about his experience as a Scientist. Dad served in the Institute of Aerospace Medicine (IAM), Bangalore is an important responsibility of training all pilots of the Indian Air Force particularly with reference to psychological challenges encountered by them in different operations. He trained them to combat such vagaries and manage their stress with an appropriate response. He was a very popular teacher among the trainees who came to IAM because of his eloquence and compassion. He also undertook research on psychological issues related to Indian Air Force personnel to improve their health and operational efficiency. Wing Commander Rakesh Sharma, an Indian cosmonaut who participated in the Soviet Space Mission in 1984 was also one of the beneficiaries of such capacity-building initiative of Dad.

-Chapter 16-

I always felt Dad could have reached greater heights had he moved internationally but he never fancied such a thing because he was a staunch nationalist and believed in being a sincere taxpayer for the welfare of the country in general.

Dad had a very humble beginning in life as he came from a poor family. He was the only member of that family to have migrated outside his native place for higher education. He was a person who lived for the moment. He never believed in amassing wealth for future use. Though he was earning a decent income from the Government, his priority was always to make himself eligible for that by serving the nation to his utmost capacity. I could not understand his views then but today I am able to assimilate them.

I am not sure if this happens only with me but I have a strange liking to the night sky. It's a wonderful feeling yearning to be up there amongst the stars like the kites. This thought reverberates within me and everything about life gets a meaning. I understood my Dad and the impact he had on me during one of these recesses. It might be just another pastime for some but for me that activity was something that defined my existence.

Slowly as Dad's hospital visits became more frequent, sadly he started showing signs of dementia. In one particular instance of the many that were to follow, Dad totally lost himself and identified himself as being in a warzone and frantically paced about outside the house. Immediately we took him to the hospital and he was put under care.

-Chapter 17-

Dad had been diagnosed with Last Stage Kidney Disease and medicines of all kinds were becoming futile. There were moments when he would recognise us and on one such occasion, he said that all of us needed a break and that we should go on a refreshing holiday. We promised him that but it never happened.

While being disoriented, he would always talk about what had happened years back while in Allahabad, Jabalpur, Delhi, Bangalore and other places wherever he had been to in his official capacity. In a way, he was transposed to that period, a sort of time travel. He was completely cut-off from the present world and barely recognised us. For him, I was the caretaker of a guest house where he was put up. In spite of losing out like this on basic cognitive skills he always longed to be somewhere near to my Mom. He felt secure at the sight of Mom. Now, this cannot be explained as to why he probably felt comfortable with Mom than any one of us. We were extremely relieved that he did not feel lonely.

In due course, he stopped watching television and reading newspapers too. He would just stare at the 'The Hindu' and keep it aside. Normally he would read the entire newspaper and if found anything interesting would make a note of it in his diary. Probably one thing that we never could imbibe from Dad was his immense knowledge of the world. Unfortunately, we did not take that opportunity to tap the wonderful storehouse of knowledge that Dad was as in the prime of my youth there were enough and more distractions. Unlike most other parents Dad never forced anything into us not because we would not heed to his words but probably because that was his principle - his way of life.

-Chapter 18-

The doctors who attended him always had high regards for him and he held them all in high esteem as well. His conversation was so rich that most of the people both medical staff and patients thought him to be a Professor. Towards the advanced stages of his illness, Dad had almost completely gone into dementia.

Every day in the evenings from his bed he would give out a lecture on the dynamics of our country with regards to the economy, politics, socio-economic development and other topics that fascinated him. One could sit down and take notes from these lectures but ironically he was totally in a disoriented state of mind hardly recognising even his close family members.

Had he wished Dad could have soared the echelons of any organisation he worked for to the topmost level but he was never ambitious. He retired as Scientist 'F', DIPR-DRDO (Defence Institute of Psychological Research – Defence Research Development Organisation). Even though his health was sinking he yearned to be updated on all things around the world. Towards the end of the year 2015, he totally isolated himself from reading, writing or interaction with us. The disease was quick to affect other organs and medications had become futile.

-Chapter 19-

During one of those unconscious states of mind, Dad had a fall but there were no signs of injury externally. We took him to AIMS but unlike earlier instances when he was immediately admitted, the doctor suggested scanning of the body. When the report came the Doctors told us that there was a minor internal injury to the head and that there was nothing that could be done and told us to take him home. It was a late Saturday evening and we got in touch with the Palliative care unit in the hospital and they agreed to come home the following week onwards to care for Dad.

For dinner, he had little food and went to bed immediately. My older brother and his wife were supposed to come the next day. We had hoped that the presence of my brother would have a soothing effect on my Dad. The next morning Dad did not wake up for breakfast though we tried to feed him. He lay on one side breathing in silently and seemed to be relaxed and peaceful.

My brother was on his way from the airport. It was then that Mom came and told me that Dad was struggling with his breath. Immediately I went to his bed and tried to wake him up. I observed Dad closely and this time the closest I have ever been to my loving father. He was indeed struggling but would not wake up from his peaceful slumber. I saw him take his last deep breath and he stopped. I knew it but I called him one more time - motionless he was resting. I called the nearby hospital for an ambulance. My brother and wife came in five minutes as the disaster unfolded. I wished Dad had waited a little longer to catch a glimpse of his first and favourite son, one last time. It seemed like I had let loose a flying kite that was with me all along. At the hospital, we were officially told of the eventuality. That was the only moment I broke down for my Dad as I clasped his cold feet very hard. This was the end of an era.

News spread and very soon the near and dear ones came home to pay homage. I kept myself aloof from the arrangements for my father's last rites because I was in deep thoughts as to how I would personally reconcile with the loss. The next day when his body was pushed to the electric crematorium at Edapally, Kochi, I remained hard-faced. My brothers and other relatives couldn't control their emotions. I do not know why but there was not even a drop of tear that came out of my eyes.

-Chapter 20-

The Covid 19 virus had hit all of us very badly and the whole world seems to be in its stranglehold. It's been several years since Dad left us and all the while I have only been trying to sing an elegy to myself - thoughts which probably could fill the vacuum he has left in my life. It was not easy at all and I have been on hard times over these years languishing in memories. I always feel that I should have given more of my time to Dad. Today as I look back I realise the solid support that he was as a father. No matter what the problem is, he would have come out with a solution.

Now as I struggle with problems at hand I can only sit and lament on having lost out on those precious moments with my Dad. Probably the only solace I could have now is reverberating his words of wisdom as I look into the endless sky with my thoughts meandering like a kite, as with a heavy heart I try not to let it snap.

Dad's was an eventful life (1939-2015). In spite of being born into a very ordinary family, he was unwilling to just give in to it. He understood the power that came along with education. With no backing at all and absolutely no guidance, it was his self-will and determination that took him places. He knew how to balance work and family both of which were his priorities. There was a lot that could be learned from the way he tackled life. As we grew up unaware of these harsh realities in life, he believed in education as the bedrock to a successful life.

Today I have the education to take the plunge but I lack that overwhelming attitude of my Dad. He had always wished that we asked him for guidance but my ignorance of those days got the better of me and that has eventually brought me to what I am now, bereft of his wise words.

About the Author

Gautam Nedumparambil Ramachandran was born in Allahabad, Uttar Pradesh. He grew up in Bangalore, Karnataka. His father worked as a scientist in the Defence Institute of Psychological Research (DIPR). He was schooled at Kendriya Vidyalaya Hebbal in Bangalore and Kendriya Vidyalaya Ernakulam, Kochi.

Gautam graduated with a Bachelor's degree in English Language and Literature from Maharajas's College, Ernakulam in 1998. He completed his post-graduate degree from Sacred Heart College, Kochi in 2000.

Gautam's wife works as a post-graduate teacher in English at Kendriya Vidyalaya. His older brother Rahul is an IT professional and Nikhil, his younger brother is a banker. At present Gautam is working as a Section Officer at Mahatma Gandhi University, Kottayam, Kerala.

www.ingramcontent.com/pod-product-compliance
Lightning Source LLC
LaVergne TN
LVHW041601070526
838199LV00046B/2088